An Illustrated Romantic Masterpiece.

Passion's Blood

Written and Illustrated by:

Cherif Fortin & Lynn Sanders

Medallion Press
Masterpiece Collection

Published 2008 by Medallion Press, Inc.

The MEDALLION PRESS LOGO
is a registered trademark of Medallion Press, Inc.

Copyright © 2008 by Cherif Fortin and Lynn Sanders
Artwork by Cherif Fortin and Lynn Sanders
Cover design by Adam Mock
Book design by James Tampa

Printed in the United States of America
Typeset in Brioso Pro

Library of Congress Cataloging-in-Publication Data

Fortin, Cherif.
  Passion's blood : Cherif Fortin & Lynn Sanders.
    p. cm.
  ISBN 978-1-60542-062-2 (alk. paper)
  1. Middle Ages--Fiction. I. Sanders, Lynn. II. Title.
  PS3556.O7494P37 2008
  813'.54--dc22

                    2008024556

10 9 8 7 6 5 4 3 2 1
First Edition

ACKNOWLEDGMENTS:

I would like to thank models Pat Lambke, Beth Orbison, and Dave Spung for their great portrayals of the characters in *Passion's Blood*. Their friendship and dedication to the project is sincerely appreciated.

A special 'hats off' to my artist/writer/actor/business partner Cherif Fortin for doing more than triple-duty. Cherif, my dear friend, you made the project great fun.

Thanks to my children Laurel, James and Jason who are always cheering me on and to my grand kids Amanda, Eli, Brianna and Mitchell who I love dearly.

And finally, thanks to our loyal fans without whose support and friendship *Passion's Blood* would truly not exist.

—Lynn

Although only two names appear on this book's cover, it takes a team of individuals to create a book like *Passion's Blood*.

I would like to thank my beautiful and devoted wife, Dawn, whose love, encouragement, and sense of humor keep me going when otherwise I would surely falter.

Thanks also to our wonderful children Kira, Kai, and Lara. Their cheerful and loving treatment of a sometimes grumpy, preoccupied Dad has earned my everlasting gratitude.

Thanks to Lynn Sanders, who entered my life as a business partner, but over the years has become best friend, confidant, mentor, and part of the family.

Lastly, many heartfelt thanks to Adam Mock, Helen Rosburg, and the professionals at Medallion Press. Your hard work and dedication have been a blessing.

—Cherif

Lady Leanna

Prince Emric

Prologue

Lord Gareth brought his sword down in a mighty arc, cleaving his assailant's upraised buckler in two and hurling him to his death from atop the palisade. He spat a bloody oath as another of the woad-painted savages, eyes as wild as a mad dog's, clambered over the merlon.

"Fall back!" Gareth shouted, even as he parried a dagger thrust and brought his blade down. There was the snap of bone and Gareth shouldered the slumping figure back over the wall. "Fall back," he roared again. "We'll be hemmed in!"

As if in echo to his words, a thunderous crash shook the fortress and the main gates leading into the yard from the gatehouse cracked, then split from the hinges. The Heldann horde raised a soul-shattering howl of triumph. With a final groan, the gates collapsed and were heaved aside by the tide of Highland warriors. The courtyard flowed crimson as the defenders fell beneath the sheer savagery of the Heldanners, who slew those standing before them with steel, primitive stone, and naked hands and teeth.

Gareth tore his gaze away from the terrible spectacle and moved along with the few of his men who still lived. As they climbed up the north tower stairs, the enemy poured over the walls behind them.

At his side a youth, blood streaming from a gash on his forehead, closed and barred the door. Others piled wood and debris to form what they knew would be but a short-term deterrent.

"Where did they come from? By God, where did they come from?" the lad babbled, eyes wide in total panic.

Gareth seized the coil of mail at the youth's neck and led him down the stone-lined corridor until he and his remaining men burst into the great hall.

"We'll make our stand here," Gareth bellowed with grim determination. His grey beard was spotted with foam, his mail awash with crimson. He wiped a bloody hand across his brow and gestured toward a group of men near the wall.

"You there, barricade the door. The rest of you, clear the center of the hall."

"This is unnatural, m'lord," said a dark-haired woodsman who had taken refuge in the fortress and fought as well as any of Gareth's own. He wiped gore from a long hunting knife. "The tribes this close to the Saber River do not fight in such numbers."

"They do today, by the blood of the Father," swore Gareth. Yesterday, men would have laughed at the suggestion of a united Highlands. Today, the disparate tribes were sundering the keep of Gallitain like kindling. "Let us pray our riders made Brimhall."

He took a quick count of the remaining defenders. Barely a score. Not nearly enough to fight their way out.

A sudden crash resounded through the stone-lined chamber as the Heldanners brought their battering ram to bear against the doors of the hall. Men moved away from the ramshackle barricade of furnishings to the center of the room as the echo of the ram filled the air with a sound like the tolling of a funeral knell. Already the boards were splitting near the edges. With gritted teeth, they awaited the inevitable, none but Lord Gareth daring to speak.

"You've done the king proud this day, men," he said, tightening the fastenings of his shield so it would not slip from his numbed arm. "Let us give these cursed Highlanders a reason to remember the name of Wareham." He lifted his bloodstained sword to the ready.

When at last the doors shattered and the barricade was forced aside, it was not to the roar of a slaughter-maddened mob, but to a silence infinitely more ominous. Dozens of clansmen, dripping with gore and panting with the exertion of their murderous fury, poured into the hall. Their faces bore wolfish grins and their steel glimmered like moonbeams as they surrounded the last defenders of Gallitain.

From their midst strode a tall and powerful figure, clad in furs and circular plates of steel sewn to a leather jerkin. His dark hair was braided around a face as wicked to behold as the sweep of the notched axe he held in his mighty grasp. His eyes sought and found Lord Gareth and he smiled, licking his lips in some private anticipation too loathsome to contemplate.

"Kill them all," he said flatly in a voice like the grinding of heavy stones. "But leave their chieftain to me."

The horde howled and rushed in.

Chapter One

"Let's rest here a moment," Leanna called, dropping gracefully to the ground and setting her grey mare free to graze in the sweet heather. "I tire of the ride."

She laughed softly to herself for, in truth, she had another reason for stopping. Running to the edge of a glade that seemed to be fashioned of dark green velvet, she threw herself down in the billowing grass, which was woven with delicate yellow wildflowers and dancing with butterflies. The burble of a brook a short distance away fell like music onto her ears.

Prince Emric smiled when he dismounted, amused that his betrothed moved with such energy though she professed to be fatigued. Although Leanna was ahead of him, it took him only a few strides to catch up with her. He knew this was a game and he was eager to play, for Leanna's passionate nature and independent spirit constantly surprised and delighted him.

Leanna's back was to him when he reached her, her red hair gleaming in the sun like wild silken ribbons.

He fell to his knees beside her, gently touching her shoulder. She turned to face him, and he saw she had undone her saffron surcoat and loosed the laces of her chemise, allowing her breasts, the color of roses and cream, to be caressed by the warmth of the sun.

Emric slid his arms around her and buried his face in her softness. Lightly he kissed her, teasing her with his lips and tongue. He leaned back to take in his lady, his heart racing at the sight of her delicate, creamy skin. In the past, they had always met in secret, in the shadows of the night when they had only firelight. Today, he rejoiced they could enjoy each other in the wild, open fields, their love lit by the pure golden sunlight.

Leanna flushed with desire as she watched Emric's eyes drift lazily over her. Helping him with her movements, she let him push the remaining layers of cloth aside. When his hands traveled up her thighs, her hips pushed forward, seeking his body. Smiling, she pressed her palm against his heart, pleased to feel it pounding with desire. Eager to inflame him as she had never done before, she quickly bared his broad shoulders to the sun.

Leanna's fingers on his skin aroused Emric and while holding her against his chest, he tossed his scarlet cape on the ground beneath them. Carefully, he laid her on the silken bed and arched his body over hers.

He ran his tongue along the seam of her lips again and again until she parted them to allow him entry. Only then were they joined in a deep, passionate kiss.

Gasping for breath, Leanna pulled back, thinking her lover could extract the very life from her with his kisses. She took his face in her hands and combed through his long black hair with her fingers as she stared intently into his smoldering green eyes.

"I am yours, my love," she sighed. Her lips pursed as a playful urge seized her anew. "You must teach me the ways of a truly sensuous woman. I want to please you like no other." Her hands traveled down his neck and chest. "Guide me," she whispered.

Emric's breath quickened as her hands roamed lower. "Oh, Leanna." He laughed softly. "You already please me beyond measure."

Rolling over onto his back, he lifted her above him, guiding her knees forward so that she straddled him. Taking her hands, he kissed her palms. Then he placed them on his belly and guided them lower and lower still.

Leanna shuddered with excitement when she realized he wanted her to caress him. She had touched him before, but only fleetingly and in the heat of passion. Now

Leanna pulled back, thinking her lover could
extract the very life from her with his kisses.

he was inviting her to explore him.

Slowly, deliberately, she encircled him with her fingers, feeling his warm skin, his shape and hardness. She bent down to him and pressed her lips to his belly.

He moaned and she felt him take her head in his hands and gently urge her farther down his body. As the crisp hair brushed over her mouth, her pulse raced with excitement. Did she dare kiss him there? She wanted this extreme and intimate connection with him.

Emric watched her, his eyes half-closed with passion. With a deep murmur, he pressed his tense body deep into the scarlet fabric beneath him, knowing he was totally in her power.

Leanna heard Emric's moans and felt the tension beneath her touch. Thrilling to the ecstasy she was building with her mouth and hands, she leaned back to marvel at his beauty.

Grasping the last of his control, Emric drew himself from the edge of release. Reaching up, he cupped her face and, threading his fingers through her hair, brought her sweet lips to his.

"My darling, I must have you," he breathed against her mouth. He slid his hand between their bodies and touched her.

Leanna moaned when she felt his touch. She buried her face in his neck and submitted to his strength.

Swiftly, Emric rolled over and fitted their bodies together. He closed his eyes and joined them with a movement of his hips. He wanted to go slowly, but his passion spurred him on as he thrust into her. The tension in his loins took his very breath away. His hands on her hips, his body sleek with sweat, he hung for a long moment on the brink of climax.

Leanna's cry sent him over the edge and he thrust into her shuddering, pulsating body one final time as she convulsed around him.

They lay together as one, their bodies wet against the damp red silk. Even their hair tangled, completing its own mating ritual.

*They lay together as one, their bodies
wet against the damp red silk.*

Finally, Leanna laughed, pushing Emric's wayward locks back from his face. "There you are," she teased. "Now I can see your handsome face." She touched the small scar in his eyebrow.

"I need never make love again." Emric sighed. "This moment was all too perfect, my lady." His dark lashes veiled the sensual fire in his eyes. He smiled and stretched like a restive lion in the heat of the afternoon sun.

Leanna smiled and held him close. She knew the depth of his passions. It was good to have him home at Brimhall Castle again.

"The date of our betrothal is rapidly approaching, Emric," she said, propping herself up on one elbow. "I think many a young lady at court will soon have cause to mourn." She traced a blade of grass over his muscular chest.

He arched a dark eyebrow. While Emric could not deny the occasional liaison, he considered his reputation as a rake to be greatly exaggerated. Truth be told, since their fathers' announcement of their intentions to join the houses of Kaherdin and Clairemonde by marrying the king's second son and Gareth's only daughter, he had remained virtually chaste. Well, he grinned to himself, at least virtually monogamous.

"I must profess my innocence, my lady," Emric said. "The idleness at court has made me victim of vicious rumors. If anyone will be in mourning, it will surely be the gallant Sir Bracchus." He traced a single finger down Leanna's neck and between her breasts. "If I am not mistaken, he holds the distinction of having been your most ardent suitor."

"Next to you," she chided. "Sir Bracchus is a dear man and it is not his fault you are so much more charming."

"And handsome," he said as his finger continued its journey over her breast.

"And handsome," Leanna agreed. "And courageous, witty, and oh . . . so much more dreadfully conceited."

She watched him shrug his shoulders noncommittally as he laughed. Since the announcement of the intended betrothal, the last year had been a confusing time. Initially, Leanna had been furious over the helplessness of the arranged marriage, but

Emric had astonished her by embracing the prospect wholeheartedly and courting her as though the union had been his own idea from the start.

Indeed, she had been flattered at the attentions of the kingdom's most eligible knight. True, his elder brother would inherit the throne, but nothing, not even a kingdom, could make life with Prince Bran bearable. Emric, on the contrary, was the stuff of every young girl's fantasy. He was intoxicatingly charming, yet noble hearted. Indomitable, yet gentle. She had grown to love him deeply. So why, she asked herself, did she continue to feel discomfort at the notion of a marriage with this man?

Suddenly she recalled her mother, Ursanne, two summers before her untimely passing. Leanna had never known her so serious as the day they traveled to Yn' Dunnall in the south of Wareham and entered the ancient circle of stones her mother said was holy. There Leanna first learned of the Ningal, the Gift, practiced for generations by her mother's people. She heard of the rites of Earth and Sea, and the homage owed the spirits of the Sky, and how at the first sign of the moon's blood, the women of Leanna's line came to the sacred stones to recite the oath before the Goddess:

Be true to the Queen of Light. True to Earth and Sea and Sky. Be true to thine own Self besides.

But these were not her beliefs, she reminded herself. She could not even recall the rest of the oath. Why should the words ring true for her now? Her own mother had renounced her Druid order for a life with her father. *Be true to thine own Self besides . . .* What would she do, she asked herself, when the time finally came to speak the words and take Emric as her husband?

Despite the delightful games she played with Emric, her trepidation mounted as the time of the betrothal grew closer. She glanced at Emric, who looked as if he were about to fall asleep. He surprised her when he spoke.

"I hope you're not beginning to doubt me, my dear."

"Of course not." She smiled, concealing a sudden pang of guilt. How could she tell him when she scarcely understood the ambivalence herself? She sat up, gathered her clothing, and brushed the wild grass from her hair. Then she stood and walked to her mare, which had wandered only a short way from where she had dismounted.

Emric regarded her quizzically, sensing that something had gone wrong with the mood their union had produced, but uncertain how best to put his concern into words.

"Have I offended you in some way, Leanna?" he asked, as he rose and donned his tunic.

She smiled reassuringly and mounted her horse, then cast a glance over her shoulder. "Not at all . . . but those storm clouds on the horizon disturb me well enough."

Emric looked past her at the dark grey band to the west that spread up from the horizon. "We had best make haste for the castle or we'll be taking our chances with that weather." When he mounted, she was already urging her horse in the direction of Brimhall.

"Aye," Emric murmured to himself. He spurred his steed onward to catch up. "Storm clouds, indeed."

Chapter Two

The keep of Brimhall Castle was alive with anticipation of the Summer Feast. In the courtyard, pages were busy hammering together huge tables to hold the many varieties of food and drink that even now were emerging from the kitchens. Smoke wafted skyward from several bonfires the men had lain to light the revelry long into the night. Giggling young girls roamed the parapets, decorating them with all manner of gaily colored trappings. Nearby, the sound of horns and pipes could be heard as bands of minstrels and jugglers began impromptu performances. No one chose to notice that the good Friar Corbin had yet to return from his inspection of the wine stored in the cellars.

Lady Leanna watched the tumult of activity from her balcony in the Green Tower, so named because of the ivy that clothed it. She had returned from her ride hours ago and, to the relief of her governess Mirabel, had bathed and abandoned her dusty riding clothes in favor of a festive gown. Mirabel had departed for the kitchens, promising trouble for any slackers, and left Leanna to study the North Gate in the breezes of the early evening. The storm clouds she had seen on her ride passed with only a light showering of rain and she found the ensuing coolness refreshing.

The sight of the massive stone gateway made her recall the many times Emric had ridden beneath it on campaigns to the west. Every time they had parted, he had flashed his best smile for her, adding a wink, as though he knew with all certainty that he would return. And he always had returned, riding through that giant portal atop his charger, the wind tangling his long dark hair around his handsome face, his eyes searching for her on her balcony.

Leanna's heart beat nervously as she thought of her father, who had sent her away to the relative safety of Brimhall while he defended the frontier from his holding at Gallitain. Despite the motherly attention Mirabel lavished upon her, Leanna missed him and yearned to see him again, though she admitted conflicting emotions when she remembered how he and King Morien had reveled loudly at the idea of grand-children. She flushed at the memory. Would she have no say even in this, the most personal of all decisions? she asked herself.

A commotion in the yard below interrupted Leanna's reverie as two men came into view and faced off. Both were hard limbed, broad shouldered, and clad in finery, but the resemblance ended there. One was clean shaven with closely cropped tawny hair and brilliant blue eyes. The other was dark, with a thin beard emphasizing the hard line of his mouth. Black hair framed a face made rugged from years of campaigning. Leanna recognized him as none other than Prince Bran, Emric's elder brother and heir to the throne.

A group of men crowded around the two and Leanna could hear the fair man shout an accusation.

"You are ill mannered, Your Grace," he cried with the heat of youth. "Should you not proffer an apology, I will demand satisfaction." His gloved hand went to the hilt at his side.

"Come then, Sir Owen, and satisfy your honor."

Leanna gasped at the hissing tone of Bran's reply and saw Owen hesitate to draw his sword.

"I cannot engage Your Grace in single combat," he finally said, apparently resigning himself to accept Bran's insult.

"Have no fear, Sir Knight." Bran emphasized the last words as though to ridicule the younger man. Then he turned and addressed the crowd that had gathered around.

14

"Let no man present hold falsely against Owen that he acted against his oath as a knight in engaging in this duel of honor. Be I prince or no. Unless"—he paused, eyes alive with menace, his lips curled in a grin—"unless, of course, it is cowardice that binds him."

At that final affront Owen drew his blade and both men adopted a fighting stance.

The combatants circled one another in a slow search for an opening. Bran's blade was a thin line held low, an invitation for Owen's strike. Owen raised his weapon and thrust. Steel crashed against steel, the sound ringing throughout the yard as Leanna watched in mute horror.

Suddenly, she heard Owen cry out as one of Bran's swift parries knocked him off balance. The prince's blade whipped out, sending a dark red line across the blond knight's cheek. Owen's hand went up to his face and came away dripping blood. With a curse, he pulled a fighting dagger from a sheath at his belt.

Leanna's spine became icy as Bran broke into hideous laughter, unclasping his black cape and holding it loosely with his free hand. Owen drove forward savagely, cutting back and forth in wide arcs with his sword. Bran was hard-pressed, barely able to dodge his opponent's desperate strokes, but when Owen lunged forward with his dagger, Bran brought the cape up with a skillful movement and tangled the knight's weapons.

Then, spinning in a tight circle, Bran whipped his blade across the back of his adversary's knee. The stroke split Owen's flesh open and sent him in a heap onto the cobblestones.

Bran circled his crippled opponent, who now lay helpless in a ball of agony. As Bran lifted his blade for the final blow, his gaze found Leanna standing on her balcony.

She stood frozen, unable to dislodge herself from Bran's penetrating stare. He had looked at her many times before with blatant desire, covetous lust naked in his gaze. But now she saw something else in his eyes, something that frightened her more than his wanton leers ever had. It was the look of exhilaration at the agony he had wrought.

Unwittingly she knew his thoughts as if he had spoken aloud. *My adversary's pain shall redeem me in your eyes.*

Bran sheathed his blade and extended his hand to a man at the edge of the crowd. "Bring me my whip," he said.

On a nearly subconscious level Leanna had been aware that she, too, possessed the Ningal, her mother's hereditary gift. Many times she had received impressions of others' thoughts, but the impressions had always been unbidden and vague. Never before had they been so strong.

Now, still locked in Bran's frightful stare, she understood that through her gift the eyes of the mind had shown her his anger and hatred. She could no more detach herself from the cruel savagery of his inner being than she could turn away from his vicious eyes.

The attendant deposited a thick coil of black leather in the prince's open palm. Bran's fingers curled around the whip and then, with a flick of his wrist, it unfurled to its full length.

Leanna gasped as the whip lashed forward like a monstrous snake, striking Sir Owen on the back of his legs. She covered her ears at his high-pitched scream, but could not shut herself away from the horror that was unfolding beneath her balcony. Again the whip cracked, sounding even louder, then again . . . and again.

Bran drew back for another vicious blow. He was stopped short when a mailed fist seized his wrist.

Emric's voice was furious as he yanked Bran around to face him. "No sooner do we lose one enemy, dear brother, than you must seek out a new one amongst our allies." Emric signaled a squad of men-at-arms to disperse the crowd.

In the confusion of the duel, Leanna had not seen Emric approach. Now her heart raced at the sight of her love.

"It was fair combat, Emric," Bran spat at his brother, yanking his arm free. "Sir Owen challenged and I accepted as befits the laws of chivalry."

"Of course," said Emric, narrowing his eyes. He took a step closer. "And how does chivalry regard the torture of an unarmed man? I have ridden into many a battle with Sir Owen, of the noble house of Loriel, and I know that he is a just and brave knight. Your actions this day have cost our father a dearly needed vassal."

"The king has knights aplenty, brother, and no need for one who fought so rashly," Bran said. "Or perhaps you think me a liar when I say that it was he who cast the challenge?"

"If Owen yet lives, it is he I shall ask for the truth."

The brothers regarded each other for a long, dangerous moment. Then Bran smiled and took a step back.

"There were witnesses, brother. In any case, I take my leave of you. All this fighting has given me a fierce appetite." He inclined his head ever so lightly in a mocking bow. "I trust the matter is at an end." Spinning, Bran strode out of the courtyard, courtiers trailing behind him.

Emric watched his brother disappear through the inner gate, then ordered his men to attend the fallen Sir Owen. A slight motion from above caught his eye; he looked up to see Leanna. Though she had clenched her hands tightly before her, even from this distance, he could see she was trembling. He sent her a reassuring smile, but she only stared at him in response.

Chapter Three

herald's trumpet marked the official beginning of the Summer Feast. Villagers had already filtered into the castle courtyards from outside the walls. Now they milled about with the jugglers and performers, and partook with abandon of the heaping platters of food and freely flowing ale.

Lady Leanna, still preoccupied by thoughts of the combat in the yard, waited in the great hall as the royal procession entered though the massive, iron-bound doors. King Morien, his sons at either hand, led the assemblage. Attendants scurried aside as the mighty king, known to all as the Lion of Wareham, took his place at the head table.

"Let the feast begin!" he commanded and emptied his jewel-encrusted goblet as the assembled nobles cheered.

At once, the hall exploded into activity. Pages entered, carrying dishes piled high with meats. Leanna wondered how she would be able to eat even a bite. A servant, struggling under the weight of a huge platter, deposited a large steaming bird, decorated with its own brilliant plumage, onto the table.

"A peacock!" exclaimed Count deBracie with delight, edging forward to examine it in amazement. "King Morien has truly spared no expense this day. Such beasts roam only well beyond the Inland Sea."

Leanna paid the count little mind. Instead, she leaned against Emric, anxious to hold him closely. Propriety demanded otherwise and she had to be satisfied with a lingering brush against his body.

"You look ravishing, my love," he whispered, smiling warmly at the sight of her.

She, too, looked at Emric with approval. He was magnificent in his dark chausses and a rich blue tunic, finely embroidered in gold. She wished they were alone so she could bury her face in the dark hair that fell in thick waves around his strong shoulders. He laughed at someone's comment and, as the sound of his mirth filled the hall, Leanna felt her own spirits lifting.

She knew it was sometimes whispered at court that many lords regretted Emric had not been born the eldest. Bran's sullen moods alienated a good many of Wareham's most powerful nobles, and Leanna was certain the incident with Sir Owen would only widen the rift. Even the most oblivious of courtiers knew the uncertainty with which nobles regarded the succession. But Emric would not suffer the subject to be mentioned in his presence, and Leanna had never pressed him to discuss it.

"So, Leanna," began King Morien, dabbing at his chin with the edge of a silken sleeve. "How fares your noble father?"

She smiled, as grateful for the king's interest as for the respite it promised from yet another of Count deBracie's anecdotes.

"He is well, my lord, although I have not had word from him in some time."

The king reached across Emric to pat her hand. "Take heart, child. Undoubtedly his duties in Gallitain keep him preoccupied. It is a severe responsibility Gareth has undertaken in securing the hinterlands, you know."

He smiled reassuringly and Leanna warmed at the unexpected display of affection. "Thank you, Your Majesty," she managed, wishing she could voice her fears.

She often worried for her father, who commanded a lonely outpost on the frontier of Wareham, where the fertile lands surrounding the Saber River had begun to attract droves of settlers. Clashes with the barely civilized tribes of the Heldann Highlands were common, but her father had insisted their lack of organization made them more of a hindrance than an actual threat.

She reached for the goblet of wine set between her and Emric when she caught sight of a commotion at the entrance of the hall.

Captain Aelfric, the veteran commander of Brimhall's garrison, stood framed by the massive, metal-bound doors. He entered the hall and formally saluted, countenance as stern as ever.

"What is it, good captain?" queried the king loudly, as all the guests looked toward the man.

The soldier took another step forward. "There are heralds without to see Your Grace. They are Heldanners, and they carry the banner of diplomacy."

A great clamor arose from the assemblage at the news. King Morien, his noble features fixed in deliberation, raised his hand, calling at once for silence.

"Bring them in, Aelfric. Let us hear what tidings these messengers bear."

Leanna pressed close to Emric, whose apparent disquiet heightened her own. Never before had Highlanders ventured from their wilds in the region men dubbed Heldann, except to raid the farmsteads and settlements along the border. Their appearance here was distressing. She cast a glance at Bran, who seemed equally intent on the developments.

Four men, armed with sword and round shield and clad in the peculiar, banded armor and furs of the Heldann warriors, entered the hall. The stoutest held a tall spear from which a dark blue banner depended. They glared at the group of feasting nobles with something akin to disgust.

"Morien, King of Wareham!" one of them shouted, striding ahead of the rest.

"We have come in the fashion of your people to bear a message from King Lorccan of Heldann."

"King Lorccan?" asked Morien. "Why has this king not made himself known to us before?"

"I am Angvard, war-leader of Clan McQuillan, come recently under the banner of King Lorccan," said the Heldanner spokesman, "as have all the clans west and north of your borders. My lord has not had cause to acknowledge your holdings until now."

King Morien ignored the slight. "Say your message," he commanded.

"The lands you once called Gallitain now lie in ruin by Lorccan's hand and the might of his warriors," the Heldanner stated plainly.

Leanna gasped in horror, deaf to the clamor of disbelief from the assembled nobles.

"Along the river you call Saber," the barbarian continued, "your farmsteads burn and the women bewail the loss of their weakling men. The earth is red with the blood of your dead." To emphasize his point, he unfurled the standard that had hung in the hall of the fortress at Gallitain and threw it to the ground.

Prince Bran stood, his face drawn in lines of outrage, and reached for his sword, but his father stopped him with a gesture. The king stood in turn, narrowed eyes flashing with anger.

"So let there be war between our peoples. Go and tell this Lor—"

"There is more!" shouted Angvard, heedless of his blatant arrogance before the king. "You are commanded to withdraw from your holdings west of the foothills we call Agarra, leaving those lands to be administered as Lorccan chooses. You may continue to rule the remainder of Wareham, provided you agree to pay tribute, the manner of which shall be decided by my master.

"I am further instructed to say that if you fail to obey, you will all surely die. As we swept down upon Gallitain, reaping your warriors like sheaves of ripe grain, so shall we descend on Brimhall itself, and there will be none amongst you to stop us."

Prince Bran drew his sword in a flash. "My lord father," he cried. "I beg you, let me skin these worthless barbarians and send their hides back to their dog of a king.

"My lord father", Prince Bran cried. "I beg you, let me skin these worthless barbarians and send their hides back to their dog of a king."

The only tribute they'll take from Wareham is a sword through the belly—"

King Morien sent a balled fist crashing against the table. "As long as I draw breath, not a single league of my kingdom will I yield to this barbarian, Lorccan. Tell this insolent chief that if it is war he wishes, then he has found it. He will count his tribute in Wareham arrows, one for each of his cowardly followers.

"Now go, before I lose control over these men and must watch them cut you down."

Angvard laughed harshly. He and his escort clattered out of the hall.

The king lowered his great lion's head to his breast. "There will be no tourneys on the morrow," he proclaimed. "We shall have real war soon enough."

The sudden din of activity in the hall drowned the sound of Leanna's grief-stricken weeping.

Chapter Four

Emric dismissed his squires to linger a moment in his apartments. He crossed the room to the giant hearth where a dying fire sputtered and crackled. Lost in thought, he poured himself a cup of wine from a decanter that stood nearby and drank deeply, mulling over the words of the past hour.

"This Lorccan fancies that declaring his mastery over a few savage tribes will earn him the fellowship of kings," his father had said in the council chamber above the main hall. "He shall come to curse his foolish ambition."

A general hum of approval had risen from the assembled lords as they bent over their maps, while Aelfric moved small wooden figures about the charts, plotting the movements of Wareham's troops.

"Never fear. We shall crack this impudent fool like a nut, Father," Bran cried, pounding his huge, clenched fists upon the table. "I swear to you."

"Swear us no oaths," Emric interrupted his brother. "This Highlander is no weakling for us to easily break and sweep aside. Forget not that he has already taken Gallitain, no mean feat even for the mightiest army."

One knight protested, but the king silenced him. "Emric speaks truly. It would be a grave mistake to underestimate him, else one day his banner may fly from Brimhall's very walls. Aelfric," he said, turning to the grizzled captain. "What say you?"

"I will not lie, sire. We are outmanned." He cleared his throat. "We have but a few hundred here, with less than a hundred horses. Prince Bran's garrison at Karvoie has twice that number and Loriel has three hundred here." He pointed to a spot on the map. "But it will take days to assemble them. If we had but a few weeks to raise our levies . . ." He gestured helplessly.

"Emric." The king turned to him. "You have fought at Gareth's side against this foe before. What make you of them?"

"When we forced the Highland clans back beyond the Saber, they were disorganized savages with naught more than bronze swords and spears who did little but raid border villages. If this Lorccan has power enough to unify the clans, they will be formidable, for they are vast in number and fight without fear of death.

"To worsen matters, the hills and forests around Gallitain are to their liking. They can sally out at their leisure to slaughter along our borders."

"But they will not be content with Gallitain," Bran said. "It was plain enough that Lorccan desires all of Wareham."

Emric nodded and a silence descended upon the council chamber as the king bent his head in thought. When King Morien finally spoke, his voice was loud and clear.

"Aelfric, send half a dozen of your fastest men to Loriel with orders to march half his number to Gallitain and levy what he can from his vassals and peasants. Bran, leave a detachment at Karvoie and march the remainder to Brimhall for our protection."

He looked to Emric then and it seemed for a moment his voice caught deep in his throat. "Now to you, my son. Would that another be at my command, but I must ask this of you. Take Brimhall's men and ride with all haste to Gallitain. The enemy's number is great, but you must engage and detain them until reinforcements can reach you. Else we are completely unprotected."

All eyes on him, Emric bowed. "I shall not dishonor you, Father. I shall give a good accounting of Wareham courage." The words were so easy to say, yet Emric knew what living up to them meant.

King Morien nodded. "All of you to your tasks. Good fortune and Godspeed to you all."

As the assembled men had filed out of the chamber, the king had reached out and gently placed his hand upon Emric's shoulder. Nothing more was spoken between them. Nothing more was necessary.

Emric tore his gaze from the embers of the fire. His preparations were nearly complete, but his heart was heavy. He had fought often enough against the Highlanders, had

seen them slake their steel in the blood of men, and heard their feral howls of joy at the slaughter. He had contemplated upcoming battles a dozen times but never a battle that could well mean suicide. Fear hung about him like a black cloak.

The prince stormed from his chamber and traversed the long stone-lined corridors of Brimhall. Soon he found himself before a stout wooden door he had seen a hundred times before but which now appeared before him as though it were the first, or the last. He cast open the heavy portal and stepped inside.

Leanna sat at her window, and in the stillness of her chamber he could hear the clatter of armed men in the courtyard below. When she turned to face him, he saw she had been weeping, and bitterly Emric recalled it was mere days ago he had vowed to her nothing would ever separate them again. He wondered if some part of him had known he could never keep the oath.

Crossing the chamber in three great strides, he took her into his arms. Even as he crushed her to him, it seemed his arms were already letting her go.

Leanna pressed her lips against Emric's as his hair fell across her cheeks and mingled with her hot tears.

"I cannot bear it that you are leaving me, my love," she whispered. "If my father is dead, you are all I have left."

He looked down at her lovely face. "I must." Lifting his hands to wipe away her tears, he forced a smile onto his lips. "But I will come back to you. I swear it."

She shook her head and new tears slid down her face. "You swore that you would never leave me. How can I believe you now?"

"Have faith, my beloved." He took her hands and pressed them against his chest. "Listen to my heart beat and know that it beats only for you. How could I not come back to you?"

She could say nothing, her eyes wide and full of doubt. Emric wondered if she somehow saw the fear his confident words concealed.

Leanna looked at Emric. He was smiling and his words were easy and reassuring, but she felt such disquiet in her heart, for the Ningal revealed his innermost thoughts

as clearly as if he had spoken. She brought her hands up and gripped his hair, seeking to reaffirm her love in the face of their fear.

"Make love to me, Emric." Her voice was urgent. "Make love to me so that I will feel your body against mine when you are gone." Her voice caught. "So that I will have *something*."

Emric swept her up in his arms and carried her to the bed.

Undoing the fastenings of her robe, he quickly pushed it back and filled his hands with her soft curves. She arched up toward him, her fragrant skin warm against his face.

They lay together forgetting for just a moment the sadness within them. Lifting his head, he began to touch her. His hands mapped her body as if he could memorize her every curve with his fingertips. He looked down at the fiery hair swirling around her shoulders and cascading across her breast. The ache in his heart grew. . . .

"Come to me now, my love," she whispered brokenly. "Please. I want to feel your body."

Emric held her for a short time. He made to rise from the bed, but her arms held him from leaving.

"I shall remember you as you were in the meadow, happy and carefree in the warm sunshine." He took her face in his hands and kissed her once. When a blue ribbon alighted against his hand, he pulled it from her hair.

He swung his legs to the floor and pulled on his boots before she could protest. When he stood, something in his eyes made him seem suddenly cold and more un-yielding than ever before. As though her very presence challenged his resolve, he walked out of the chamber without a final word.

When Emric reached his chamber, he found his squires waiting to gird him with his heavy armor plates. He moved to the fire and lifted both arms for them in the time-honored ritual. "Dress me," he instructed flatly.

Some time later, he mounted his charger in the courtyard below. The men were waiting, assembled in ranks. He glanced up at the Green Tower and found Leanna's balcony. Her room was dark, but he knew she would not sleep this night. He held her blue ribbon to his lips and said a silent good-bye.

"Company, ready," he ordered, touching spurs to the stallion beneath him. "Move out."

Chapter Five

Sleep was long in coming to Leanna. She lay awake for many hours, praying and weeping in silent torment, both for her father and for Emric. She could not believe the news that her father was dead. There was no tangible proof for it, but his prospects were slim. If he had been captured by his enemies, there would have been a ransom. She clung to hope, even as she knew it might one day exacerbate the pain.

The bitter ache within her was made even more unbearable by her farewell to Emric. He tried to conceal it from her, but she had seen into his heart and knew the truth of his mission: *My love, would that fate decreed a chance for us.* She cursed the gift that revealed his mind, for it left her feeling as though she were already grieving for him.

When she woke, she found her face wet. The tears followed her even in her sleep. The fire was dead, the room dark but for a beam of moonlight that filtered through the window. She sighed and wiped the moisture from her cheeks.

Suddenly, she shuddered, seized by the feeling that she was not alone.

A cry formed on her lips but was stifled by a great, meaty hand. Sharp terror gripped her as the assailant caught both her wrists in his free hand with a strength that defied her imagination.

"Quiet, my sweet."

She heard the voice as the dark figure loomed over her like a specter from a nightmare.

"I've come to claim my prize."

With a menacing chuckle he leaned back, moonlight illuminating his face, and Leanna recognized her assailant.

"Bran!" She heard the terror in her own voice.

She kicked at him and struggled vainly to free her hands, but her efforts were as puny to Bran as those of a child. Finally, her movements annoyed him, for he swore and struck her across the mouth with the back of his hand.

The blow stung and filled Leanna's mouth with the bitter taste of her own blood. Unwanted tears filled her vision and dropped from her lashes.

"Enough of that, my pretty," he hissed, freeing something from his belt. "Fight me again and my next blow shall be worthy of a man."

Leanna remembered the sight of Sir Owen on the ground and Bran's laughter as the blood poured from Owen's crippled body. The horror of Bran's thoughts that day flashed into her mind. She wondered how she would be able to defy him.

Leanna struggled vainly against the filthy cloth with which he gagged her. Bran seized her by the waist, lifting her easily off the bed and onto his shoulder. As he flung her up, Leanna became aware of two shadows on the floor near the door. The shapes resolved into the bodies of guardsmen, black pools of blood spreading from them. Leanna screamed, but only a muted guttural sound escaped her.

Bran strode into the dimly lit hall, his squirming bundle an easy weight on his mighty shoulders. Several of his bondsmen were in the gloom of the hall, their blades drawn.

"Come," Bran whispered hoarsely to one of them. "I have what I desire."

They made quickly for the stairs, but came short as a naked blade emerged from the darkness.

The cloak-wrapped figure of King Morien stepped before them, his sword held high at the ready. He studied the men around him and when he spoke his voice was

steady and strong.

"Sleep did not come tonight, so I paced the ramparts. Then I heard a cry. Now I find this mischief? What have you done here, Bran?" When only silence followed, he roared, "Answer me, boy!"

Bran slowly lowered Leanna to the floor.

"Destiny smiles upon me this night, it seems," he said. "But what's this you've brought for me, Father? The point of your blade?" He drew his own sword in an instant, though his stance remained relaxed, nonchalant.

Morien stood tensely, watching the crowd of armed men. Then his eye caught the pool of blood that had spread beyond the door of Leanna's chamber.

"Whom have you killed this night?" he shouted. "And you dare to draw steel against your king?"

"Oh, I dare much more than that," the prince responded icily. He made a short, quick gesture toward his henchmen. "Seize him!"

As one, Bran's men-at-arms rushed forward. The first reached the figure of the king sidelong, fouling his sword arm as it rose in defense. The desperate struggle lasted but a few tense moments before Morien was overwhelmed, his steel clattering uselessly to the stone floor.

"What treachery is this, Bran?" the king asked, his composure regained. "You go too far in this . . ."

"I do as I have always done. I do as I please." Bran gripped the king's jaw roughly in his hand, staring coldly into his father's narrowed eyes. "And you would do well to change your tone. I am no longer your whelp to be spoken to thus.

"It would please you to know my designs?" Bran's tone mocked his father. "Then I shall give you this last comfort.

"I have planned this moment with the mind of the true conqueror, for I look ahead for years where others look mere days. Lorccan came to me, his men piling furs at my feet to win my favor, and I knew he could be controlled by his ambition.

"I made him king, first over his neighbors, then the whole of the Heldann Highlands. I supplied him with steel weapons and armor, schooled his men and horses. My hand guided him throughout, even as he swept out of his lands to lay flame and slaughter on Gallitain.

"But the cursed barbarian's pride burns hotly in his breast such that he issued you a formal challenge. Had the dog bided his time, you would have learned his name at the point of his blade within these very walls.

"No matter, for the end shall be the same. My army is ready to march, and with the garrison gone from Brimhall, all resistance will be easily crushed. Once Lorccan has made but a memory of my dear brother, I shall send him along the coast until his hordes are too weak to oppose me. They will have served me well."

Morien shook his head sadly. His tone was incredulous. "Betrayal? But why? In time, this would all have come to you."

"Would it? I have no intention of ruling as you do, Father, feebly scraping this way and that to appease those beneath me. I would have that upstart Loriel in the south and Emric courting the nobles away from me. I would inherit civil war. Better to strike now at my enemies and take by force the whole of what is rightfully mine."

The king paled in the face of his son's ambition. His gaze went to Leanna, who lay bound against the wall.

Bran read the unspoken question in his father's eyes. "Leanna will make a fitting queen for me when I sit on the throne of Wareham. She will be my final victory."

"This is madness . . . madness," the king muttered. Without warning he cried in alarm, "Guard! Gua—"

Bran clapped his hand over the king's mouth, silencing him at once.

"It is fortunate you come to my sword now, Morien, instead of on the battlefield. Without your leadership to rally your troops, my triumph is assured. I bid you

farewell, Father. Know that all you have amassed in your lifetime will, indeed, be mine and that your beloved Emric will soon join you in death."

With a lightning-quick motion of his arm, Bran lashed out. His sword sank to the hilt in the mighty king's chest.

A mix of surprise and sorrow passed over Morien's face before he crumpled to the floor. Leanna's muffled screams echoed from the walls.

"Take her," ordered Bran as he wiped sweat from his face with a trembling hand. "We ride for Karvoie."

He watched as his father's lifeblood ebbed in a pool at his feet, until he heard the sound of armored men descending from the stair above. He fled for the yard below, unable to sheath his blade for the cursed shaking of his hands.

Chapter Six

Prince Emric studied the silhouette of Castle Gallitain in the distance. The fires of the Heldann watchmen were visible through the crenellations as heavy clouds began to obscure the midnight sky.

Emric and his men were near exhaustion, having ridden at a merciless pace for days through lands ravaged by fire and pillage. He ordered meals delayed until pickets were set and the camp secured against attack. He had learned long ago the value of attention to detail when on the battlefield.

Emric shrugged off his dusty cloak and tunic, seized a nearby bucket of water, and lifted it, sending the cool liquid splashing against his tired body. It did not soothe the fires raging within him.

He turned wearily into his tent and dropped onto the straw-filled mattress. Fatigued as he was, sleep still avoided him. Heavy thoughts of the morning plagued him, for he knew they must face an opponent who not only greatly outnumbered them but was better prepared and rested. He searched his mind over and over for some advantage but could find none. The wisest course was to avoid open combat as long as possible unless the enemy marched for the interior.

But Emric knew they would have to fight, for the Heldanners had no reason not to ride out at first light to crush him and his force like so many bothersome insects.

He yearned for the peace of sleep, to leave the heavy responsibilities behind, if only for a brief time, and to escape into Leanna's warm embrace. At last, the prince slipped into the dark haven of his dreams and there he found her . . .

Leanna's chamber was warm in the glow of candles and smelled faintly of sweet freesia. Emric heard her moan as she stretched back across her bed of soft, deep furs. Her hair spread across the velvet pillows, gleaming red in the dim light.

Reaching up, she tangled her fingers in his dark hair and guided him down to her waiting body.

Raising himself on one arm, he lowered his head to her breast and kissed the soft roundness. Her skin was like velvet and smelled of spring flowers. He pressed his face firmly against her breast, inhaling her fragrance. Arousal tightened wantonly in his belly. Shifting her legs apart, he stroked his hands up the length of her smooth ivory thighs.

Slowly, he let his mouth kiss its way down her body, over her belly, and down to the soft copper curls below. His fingers traced her delicately, parting the silken curls to reveal her. His tongue licked out teasingly.

Her cry of pleasure as his mouth caressed her told him how well he could please her.

Shifting back upward, he suckled at her breast while his fingers entered her. Gently, he moved his fingers back and forth until he saw his desire reflected in her eyes. Her head rolled from side to side on the pillow, and her hands tangled feverishly in his hair before they slid down his back, her nails sinking into his flesh.

"Please, my love . . ." she whispered. "Do not deny me."

Her words and her breathless sighs excited him beyond measure. He felt her hand reach out to find him. Freeing him, she brazenly caressed him as her hungry lips sought his. No, he would not deny her.

The last vestiges of clothing were quickly cast aside. From the corner of his eye he caught the reflection of his crimson cloak on his armor and briefly shuddered, for it gleamed like newly shed blood. A small blue ribbon curled on the ground next to it.

He looked back to Leanna, who lay beneath him, her lovely body naked in the half light of the fire. She nestled into the furs, arms reaching for him, legs parting for him. He lowered his body, hard with desire to possess her.

She gasped when he entered her. Her arms twined round his neck and she opened her mouth for his tongue as she had opened her body to accept him. He joined their mouths as he had joined their bodies, tasting her sweetness.

He filled her and in return, the emptiness within him was also filled. He felt her body move beneath him, and his hunger for her was so overpowering he feared he would hurt her with his superior strength. He fought against the powerful instinct that took hold of him, the timeless urge of the male animal to conquer and consume.

She lay beneath him as delicate as a flower, her hands gripping his shoulders with surprising urgency. "Emric, my prince . . ." Her breath was ragged. "I want to feel all of you."

"I must have you," he moaned. His body tensed and arched, then he thrust into her again and again, holding nothing back. He was drowning in a torrent of desire.

"Leanna . . . oh, Leanna." He murmured her name over and over, his mouth hot on her skin. His body set a pounding rhythm deep inside her. Both hands on her breasts, he caressed her nipples and she moaned with pleasure at the ardor of their loving.

He felt her tighten and pulse as she approached the brink of ecstasy. When he felt her climactic moment, he, too, exploded and then felt nothing but his own blinding release.

When the flood of sensations receded, he opened his eyes. A motion caught his attention and he looked to the nearby pile of clothing and stained armor, which now, strangely, had grown to include broken weapons. It glowed with reddish light and to Emric's horror, blood began flowing from it.

Emric's pulse pounded as a hopeless terror welled up inside him. The dream had become a nightmare.

A dark figure ran into the tent, the sounds of battle mounting from without. "They're here, my lord!" the man shouted in a panic-stricken voice. "The Heldanners attack!" As he spoke the last words, he gasped and went down under a hail of arrows.

Emric clutched at his temples, unable to comprehend what was unfolding. The cloth of the tent ripped away, replaced by the fury of open battle. All around him men were dying, horses screaming as they charged, weapons clanging against armor.

He reached for Leanna, but found only the hilt of a bloodstained sword.

Emric bolted awake at the sound of horsemen entering the camp. Men were calling his name. His dream had turned so abruptly he still felt chilled and confused. Outside it was dark, and he took a moment to gather his senses.

He rose and quickly dressed before flinging aside the opening to his tent. Two riders, armor caked with dust, dismounted from their frothing steeds. They knelt before him.

"What news?" he demanded anxiously, recognizing them as men he had sent to observe Castle Gallitain.

"My lord, the enemy has left the castle and even now approaches," said the ranking warrior, pulling a grimy hand through tangled and matted grey hair.

"How many?" Emric demanded. He motioned a squire to him and, taking his water flask, proffered it to the riders. They pulled long and hard at it.

"The whole garrison, my lord," the soldier said. "Easily two thousand men, mostly afoot."

The gathering throng of soldiers and knights murmured at the report, each man realizing with certainty the narrow possibility of defeating so numerous an enemy.

Emric lowered his head in thought before he finally addressed his men. "Now is the time," he shouted, "to prove the worth of Wareham steel to those who would seek to enslave us." A thrilling moment of clarity flashed through him.

"Captain!" he called to Aelfric, who had insisted on being allowed to accompany the prince on his terrible mission. "This is what we will do."

He gave Aelfric his orders and then placed a hand on the old warrior's shoulder. "If luck is with us, the predawn gloom will conceal our meager numbers."

The captain managed a thin smile.

The camp burst into activity and at the center of it all the prince stood, his eyes turned eastward toward the enemy and his destiny.

Chapter Seven

From the copse that hid him and his men from view, Emric watched a stream run its course like a blue ribbon down a narrow ravine. The walls of the surrounding valley were high, and he understood that while this position made an ideal trap for the enemy, it could also make a tomb for his warriors. The only escape route was behind him through a range of low hills where the rest of his men lay concealed.

He took a deep breath. He could not know if Aelfric and his troops were ready, only that it was too late to change his plans.

One of the knights nearest him called softly and pointed. Emric saw the Heldanner vanguard appear out of the gloom, savages naked but for colored mud. The main host followed. Two thousand strong, their dark mass formed a deadly wall that bristled with spears and fury. Lorccan's army was a motley collection fused from a dozen different tribes, but they marched with a unity only their terrible purpose could lend.

The enemy host surged forward as Emric's desperate plan unfolded. Silently at first, but with a growing roar of pounding hooves that sounded like faraway thunder, Aelfric's men charged from their wooded hiding place. Two hundred lancers pounded into the soft, unsuspecting flank of the Heldanner column, smashing a bloody wedge into the force.

Highlanders fell beneath the charging hooves, lance tips piercing their armor. Turning, they faced the torrent of death that had descended upon them.

"Quickly," Emric shouted, signaling to sound the charge. "We must strike before Aelfric's men are cut to ribbons."

Trumpets blasted and a moment later the assembled ranks of Emric's knights began their charge. Emric spurred his destrier to a relentless gallop, pounding down the long slope toward the Heldanners as his archers loosed a whistling cloud overhead.

He lowered his lance, couching it at the ready as the enemy ranks drew nearer. His breath came in short gasps, the sound of his pulse filling his helmet with a roar. He saw the enemy's front lines go down, dissolving under the bright hail of cloth-yard shafts from the bowmen.

Then came a gigantic crash as the first of his knights rode headlong into the sea of flesh, sending lengths of razor sharp death into the lines. Horses screamed and men shouted their last as the charge crumpled into the wall of Heldanners.

Emric discarded his shattered lance and drew his sword.

He could see the two Wareham forces were nearly upon each other; the ploy had been well reasoned. As Aelfric smashed the Highlanders' flank, causing the main body to turn in response, Emric's charge fell upon the unsuspecting foe with murderous force. A good third of the Heldann column lay wounded or dead on the blood-soaked earth or was fleeing in panic into the wilds.

A Highlander ran toward Emric, howling and swinging his blade. The prince urged his destrier forward, trampling the man down, but then his mount reared as he found himself beset on all sides. Blows rang against Emric's armored thighs and clamored against his shield. Many times his blade bit into yielding flesh, and Emric soon covered with the blood of dying men.

All around him the Heldann host surged. He cursed, realizing the force of his surprise attack was now completely spent. And still he delivered blow after blow, his arm numbing with the endless repetition.

Emric fought in this way for what seemed like hours, until the tide of battle shifted away momentarily. He heard Aelfric's shout as the captain fought his way valiantly to his side. Scarlet poured from a crease in his armor near the shoulder, but his voice held triumph.

"We've cut them to the bone, my lord. God knows, 'tis more than anyone would have thought possible. But we must sound the retreat or the Heldanners will rend us to a man."

Emric started about him and saw that Highlanders were dragging armored knights from their saddles or cutting the hocks of the horses beneath them. Their numbers seemed to be swelling and he understood that his men were being surrounded.

But to flee while the battle still raged? The thought repulsed him.

"Prince Emric," old Aelfric urged. "Escape will not be at hand much longer. There is no cowardice in living to fight another day."

Emric hesitated for a moment, and then nodded. "Give the order, Captain."

He sighed bitterly, taking in the sight of the pitched battle. As he turned his horse, his eye was drawn to a circle of heavily armored Heldanner swordsmen, knee-deep in the cold stream nearby. The Highlanders were tightly packed around a tall, black-haired giant, who struck as mightily as a berserker, his great axe cleaving bone and mail alike. Something in his bearing, or in the way the warriors nearby struggled to protect him, marked him.

"Lorccan!" Emric hissed, a great rage welling up within him. In an instant he resolved to send to hell the one responsible for the death of so many even if the cost was his own life. With a shout, he spurred his mount into the thick, slashing and hewing with reckless anger.

Someone behind him yelled for him to stop, but Emric was heedless, caught in the mad, exhilarated throes of his desperate bloodlust. Men fell like ripe grain around him as his steed splashed into the stream, scattering warriors under its steel-shod hooves. He rode to his death as though to a feast, laughing and shouting until his warhorse was cut from beneath him and he careened with a mighty splash into waist-deep waters.

Emric struggled to his feet, numbly aware that others were fighting with him. He caught sight of Lorccan a mere stone's throw away and charged, pulling a dagger from his belt to replace his lost sword.

The Heldanner chief wheeled his great axe over his head, swinging it across in a blow that would surely have slain the prince were it not for his helmet, which was

sent flying from mailed shoulders. The two men collided forcefully and, at the same instant, the prince's knife punctured Lorccan's mail. A crimson tide erupted over the hilt.

Emric struggled to maintain his reeling senses as the body of his adversary slumped below the cold waters. His vision dimmed and his legs collapsed beneath the weight of his own body.

As he passed into unconsciousness, he saw the image of a red-haired girl in a field of yellow flowers. She was weeping and he felt very sad, indeed.

Chapter Eight

"God be praised, he's alive."

The voice sounded hollow and distant, and Emric could feel someone jostling him roughly.

"My lord. My lord."

Slowly he opened his eyes. The light of day was like a hammer blow to his head. An armored man he did not recognize was cradling his head, and several others stood nearby.

"My prince," the man said. "We feared the barbarian king's dying blow had slain you when you slipped beneath the waters. Thank heaven you live."

Emric could hear the sounds of battle in the distance. "Are we captured, then?" He managed the words with difficulty.

"No, my prince," the man continued, as some of the warriors laughed. "Even now the Heldann host is scattering to the winds. Their chief dead, they are making for the hills, and our stalwarts give them chase." Gently, two knights lifted Emric upright, providing him with a view of the enemy as they fled back out of the ravine in full retreat. "The day is ours, my lord. We have beaten the horde."

"Call back our men." Emric's head swam mightily, but he kept his feet. The wound in his scalp throbbed with pain. "We must take Castle Gallitain now that the Heldanners are routed. Have Aelfric organize the ranks." When no one responded, he realized all eyes had grown somber. "What is it?" he demanded.

"The captain is dead, my lord. He died protecting you from the horde when you charged Lorccan's bodyguard. He had been wounded in the first charge, but gave no indication, urging us to fight on even when we thought all hope was lost." The man suddenly seemed ashamed.

Emric was stunned by the news. Aelfric had taught him the Way of Sword and Horse as a youth. His passing left him feeling small and vulnerable. "Where?" he asked, his voice sounding hollow.

He followed the glances of the men to a place on the bank of the stream. A body lay amid dozens of others, but shrouded with a cloak in a simple gesture of respect. He stumbled toward it to grieve for his old friend.

In the span of short minutes, not a single Heldann warrior remained in the valley. Those who lived sought escape on foot, blind luck guiding some toward the freedom of the hills, others toward the marshes of the Tenair River and certain doom. Tattered banners flapped forlornly in the breeze, and bodies littered the landscape, their twisted forms jutting heavenward as though in supplication. Most lay dead or dying, moaning their last in the crimson glow of the setting sun.

The march back to Gallitain was long and difficult. Only the wounded were allowed to remain in the saddle, for the horses were exhausted and Emric feared many would founder if pressed.

The weary host arrived at Gallitain by nightfall, finding it dark and unguarded. When scouts reported that the Heldanners had abandoned their garrison, Emric ordered the wounded tended and sent parties to secure the keep.

It was late in the evening when men discovered Lord Gareth's battered body in the dungeon.

The prince hastened to the row of dank cells beneath the castle where men cradled the unconscious man as the chains that bound him to the rough cold stones were pounded loose.

"Bring blankets and water." Emric's command was sharp and urgent.

At the prince's words, Gareth's eyes opened.

"Prince Emric." Gareth's voice was a thin, sickly rattle. "And now it seems I dream even when awake." He spoke with difficulty through cracked lips that were caked with blood. His limbs were twisted unnaturally, and Emric suspected the wheel.

Gareth was the hero of Emric's youth, by whose side he had fought many a battle. Now he lay broken and defenseless in the prince's arms, suffering as no good man should be made to do. A bitter taste rose in Emric's throat at the thought of his beloved Leanna and her terrible grief were she to see her proud father so ravaged.

"Emric, Emric," Gareth repeated, his eyes staring dully before him. Suddenly the film seemed to drop away from his gaze and he was alert again. "You? Here? But the savages . . ." He grew agitated.

"Do not fret," Emric whispered, unclasping his cloak and draping it over his old friend. "The price was high, but we crushed those dogs. Gallitain is free, and you are again among friends."

"Gallitain free . . ." Gareth mimicked, his stare drifting up to the ceiling.

Emric shuddered, wondering if Gareth's mind would ever recover from his abuses. A soldier handed him a water flask and Emric held it to the older man's lips.

When Gareth had drunk his fill, Emric prepared to rise. The older man followed his movements and then suddenly reached for Emric's arm.

"My prince," he said in a voice as coarse as a millstone. "We were betrayed."

"Do not worry, Gareth," Emric reassured him. He gently pried the man's fingers from his arm. "All is well."

"No," Lord Gareth insisted, grabbing Emric's arm again with surprising strength. "We were betrayed, surprised a mere fortnight after you departed for Brimhall with half the garrison. There was no siege." His fervor grew.

"They slew us all, even the women and children, but left me as their plaything." He drew in a long, shuddering breath. "And all by the hand of your brother."

"What say you?" Emric stared at him incredulously, sure that his pitiable condition had provoked these insane words.

Defying his crippled body, Gareth struggled to sit. He clutched Emric's breast-plate.

"I have the proof of my own eyes and ears," he burst out. "As I lay chained and under the knife, the Highlander chief cursed us for kin slayers." His eyes were wide and full of pain.

"He brought a man I knew to be of Prince Bran's bodyguard before me and ordered him to ride to his master with the news that his plan had borne fruit. 'Twas worse torture for me to hear those words than any my body endured." He fell back exhausted, but kept his eyes locked with Emric's. "Bran brought these walls down as surely as any Highland steel."

Chapter Nine

It was near midnight when an exhausted Prince Emric galloped into the cobblestoned bailey of Castle Brimhall. Gareth's news of Bran's betrayal had filled his heart with anxiety over the king's safety, and he had ridden like a madman.

Men were shouting after him, descending from their posts and bearing torches, as Emric and his escort thundered past the rising portcullis of the inner courtyard. He reined in hard, vaulting from the saddle as his mount slid to a halt before a growing crowd of assembled watchmen.

"Is the king in his quarters?" he demanded of a nearby sergeant.

"I . . . I beg Your Highness to accompany me to the hall," the man stammered hesitantly. Emric realized that he wore the livery of the house of Loriel.

New fears rose within him, and he shoved past the man, making for the great hall, forgetting in his haste even to glance at his beloved Leanna's balcony.

Within moments, he strode through the heavy oaken doors of the hall, sending the metal-bound portals open with a crash. A group of men were conferring around a map-laden table. The tallest of them stepped forward, his scarlet overcoat partially concealing the gleam of mail. Emric recognized his silver hair and beard at once.

"Duke Loriel." He stepped forward. "Where is my father?"

"Prince Emric." Loriel crossed the hall and bowed before him. He stood for a long moment, steeling himself. "My prince, it saddens me to say your beloved father is dead." He placed an arm on Emric's shoulder. "All Wareham grieves at the loss."

"How?"

"The work of an assassin the very night you marched for Gallitain. None of the murderers have been found, though the Guard still searches."

The words rippled through Emric like shock waves. This had been the secret heart of his fears made reality ever since Gareth disclosed the traitor in their midst. His father . . . dead in his own castle. It was insane, and impossible, and a million other things, none of which would change the final, implacable truth. Emric felt sickened.

To keep from retching, he seized on a nagging thought.

"You said 'murderers.' Why do you speak as though more than one hand is responsible?"

"I suspect at least two men, my prince," Loriel replied, "for an attempt was made on Lady Leanna's life, as well. Her bodyguards were found slain."

"What?" Emric could scarcely believe it. "Is she safe?"

"We believe so. She fled Brimhall to the safety of Karvoie with your brother."

"By the saints!" Emric hurled a cup from the table into the fireplace, the wine hissing when it hit the flames. He whirled away, ignoring Loriel's astonished look. "Did you see them with your own eyes, Loriel?" he demanded when he had checked his fury enough to speak.

"Nay, Your Highness." Loriel's tone was cautious. "I but arrived from the coast this very morning. Riders dispatched from Gallitain a few days ago reached me with word of the siege; they had made for Brimhall but could not break through to the interior, so decided to turn southward to my holdings. I marched north immediately, intercepting the king's messengers on the road and found things as they are now."

"To whom did the Lady Leanna communicate her desire to flee with Prince Bran?"

"No one, my lord," said Loriel after a pause. "Prince Bran himself informed the chamberlain. Apparently, she had grown faint from her ordeal."

Emric rubbed his hands over his face. His exhausted mind was reeling. "Treachery most foul has undone Wareham, Duke Loriel, and her betrayer is none other than my brother." In quick, choppy words, he related what Lord Gareth had told him. "My father's murder was undoubtedly another bloody step in Bran's plan for domination. Lady Leanna despised him. She would never have gone willingly with him."

"What would you have us do?"

"We cannot wait until the rest of your garrison arrives from the coast. My brother does not know that you are here, and I suspect he will try to attack Brimhall, thinking it undefended.

"We must take the battle to him. Assemble what men you have and march toward Karvoie. I venture you will encounter Bran's army soon enough."

"We ride together, my prince?"

"No." Emric shook his head. "I shall take a dozen of our swiftest riders on a different mission. I have seen into my brother's black heart. With luck, he will deliver himself to me." With those enigmatic words, he lowered himself into the nearest chair. The fire crackled and Emric allowed its warmth to seep into his tired body.

Loriel took his leave. At the doors of the hall, he turned to face the prince. "The nobles of Wareham will not suffer the rule of a kin slayer, Emric. Such men are cursed by God. It may not be the fate you would have chosen, but the crown is now yours by right. You are king, and Wareham is well served by it."

He strode from the hall, red coat swirling behind him, leaving Emric alone with the echo of his words.

Chapter Ten

The dark spires of Karvoie loomed in the night. Built into a cliff face at the foot of imposing northern mountains, it was raised over the crumbling remains of a fortress built by conquerors forgotten in the long history of Wareham. Its bastions had withstood many sieges, and judging by the daunting sight of it, Leanna imagined it could withstand a thousand more. Around the walls, the campfires of Bran's army burned in the night.

Leanna, bound and gagged, had made the journey in a high-sided wagon roofed in canvas. Through a crack in the planks, she had spied the forests surrounding Karvoie. Disease, she recalled, had decimated the north of Wareham years ago and it seemed the land had never fully recovered. What peasants she saw were gaunt and hollow-eyed with famine. They knelt by the roadside, more in fear than tribute. It seemed to her as though she had entered the realm of the dead.

When the wagon came to rest, Bran's hands reached in and seized her shoulders. "Welcome to your new home." He laughed as he scooped her up in his powerful arms. His step was light, even cheerful, as he carried her into the fortress.

The yard was bustling with activity: grim-faced men sharpened weapons and shouted at one another while they loaded wagons with supplies. A blacksmith's hammer rang nearby. Leanna surmised that a vast host was readying to march for war.

Bran carried her down a dark stairway to a cellar where he dropped her unceremoniously onto a bed of damp, dirty straw. Faint threads of light filtered through holes in the ceiling, and moisture ran in rivulets down the stone walls. The indescribable stench threatened to overcome her as Bran roughly unbound the ropes that held her wrists.

"I hope you find these accommodations pleasant, my lady. They are as lavish as we can afford to one of your stature here in Karvoie." He bent in a mocking bow. "Soon you will again enjoy the splendor of Brimhall . . ." he paused ". . . as my queen." His mouth curved in a lecherous smile.

"I am not ignorant of the fact that you consider me a monster, but think on this." He leaned down toward her. "Your father is not dead, as you've been led to believe. He is the prisoner of my ally, Lorccan, where he will remain as long as it suits my fancy. He is alive, though those savage Highlanders have treated him most barbarously." He shook his head in mock pity. "When I am king, I could have him brought to Brimhall, if you do your part. You will accept me as you never accepted my brother. I demand not just your submission, but your sincere desire."

Leanna shrank back against the wall. Bran took her wrist and pulled her closer roughly.

"Your pretty prince is dead by now, and soon all of Wareham will be mine. After a time, you may learn to appreciate a strong hand."

He released her and left the cellar, slamming the door and drawing the bolt home with a sound that echoed like the sealing of a crypt.

The days passed like a nightmare. The damp foulness of the cellar quickly weakened Leanna, and before long she developed a persistent, racking cough. What food Bran allowed her was meager, and she guarded the stale bread and brackish water from the rats that shared her captivity.

She thought of Emric often, praying for his safety. She had no reason to believe Bran when he claimed Emric was dead, yet Bran had seemed so pleased and sure of himself. But assuming he was lying, the fact remained that no one knew where she

was. Would anyone be coming for her? Emric was fighting for his life in the border-lands, her father was captive, and the king dead. She considered escape, but even if she managed to flee the castle, she could never evade the whole of Bran's army outside the walls.

As weakened in spirit as she was in body, she took to throwing her food to the rodents; starvation was a slow death, but preferable to a lifetime of Bran's defilement.

She fell into despair, sobbing until it seemed her tears were spent. Then, like a ray of morning sunlight, reason filtered through the dark of her anguish. She thought again of Emric and remembered his bravery and strength. He would tell her that yielding her body was not the same as surrendering her spirit. He would wish her to endure and to avenge the evils Bran had committed.

She would be strong, Leanna resolved. She would be cunning. Duplicity and guile would be her shields. And vengeance would one day be hers . . .

Leanna awoke one morning to a thunderstorm, rain pouring in thin streams from the holes in the ceiling. She had crawled, shivering, into a corner where a measure of dryness remained when the door swung open noisily and Bran descended into the cellar.

He found Leanna on her straw pallet and lifted her roughly to her feet. "How fares your fiery temper today, my lady?"

Only a pleading, submissive gaze greeted him. "This is most unexpected," he said, lifting her chin with his forefinger. "And delightful."

Leaning forward, he kissed her. When she offered no resistance, he crushed her to him in a greedy embrace.

He stepped back at last, eyes alive with lust. Leanna looked away from the evidence of his blatant arousal.

"I am well pleased to see that you are as intelligent as you are beautiful. I did not expect you to bow to reason so soon." He twisted his hand in her hair and pulled her to him.

Leanna did not fight him as he kissed her mouth and throat. She forced herself to lift her hand and caress his face, urging him to greater passion.

Bran swept her up and placed her on the crude, wooden table that stood in the middle of the cellar. Breath uneven with desire, he seized her breast in a rough caress and tore at her clothes.

Leanna closed her eyes, fearing that her glance would betray her revulsion. Bran forced her legs open and thrust his still-covered manhood against her. He pinched her nipples and she cried out with the sudden pain. She heard him make an approving sound and knew he had taken her cry for one of pleasure.

Leanna fought back the urge to resist him. Desperately, her mind searched for a haven where she could flee from the impending rape. Emric's image rose to her mind and she clung to it as her last hope.

She recalled how he would seek her out in her chamber while the castle slept. She remembered the thrill of the telltale creak of her door opening. Sometimes he stood at her bedside for long minutes, staring down at her nakedness.

"What are you gazing at, my prince?" she had asked once.

"I am drinking in your beauty, Leanna, so that it will always be with me."

"Is it enough for you simply to behold?" she had teased him. Staring into his eyes, she slowly pushed away the blanket from her body until she lay fully exposed to his gaze. "It is not enough for me."

Inflamed by her words, her half-shy, half-brazen action, he unlaced his clothes and pressed his aroused body against hers.

His hands caressed her and his fingers slid between her thighs, finding her ready. He quickly joined their bodies in a languid thrust, then stilled until she thought she would go mad with anticipation.

She moaned for mercy. "Please, Emric . . ."

A sudden fierce slap across the face shattered the haven of her memories. Her eyes flew open and she saw that Bran's face was contorted with fury.

"You called for Emric," he spat.

"N-no," Leanna stammered. "I am yours . . ."

"I warned you," he shouted and hit her again. "You will be mine without all pretenses, or your father will suffer for it."

He stepped back from her, his arousal gone, and Leanna closed her eyes as relief vied with a sense of regret for her carelessness.

"Do not think for one moment, Leanna, that you cannot be made to suffer as well," he snarled.

He opened the cellar door and called out to a servant. "Ready her. We march for Brimhall in one hour."

Leanna gathered her skirts and returned to the dry corner of the cellar. For the first time in days, the tears did not come to mingle with the rain.

Chapter Eleven

Leanna huddled, shivering against the frigid night air. Vainly, she pulled at the hempen rope that bound her to the stout central pole of Bran's pavilion.

In silence she had suffered the indignity of a day's march slung across a horse's rump, a punishment Bran had decreed for her indiscretion. Every bone in her body ached from the ordeal.

The whole of the prince's army had marched until long after sundown, driven by Bran's eagerness to attain Brimhall. When darkness made travel too treacherous for horse and wagon, it was with near petulance that he ordered his men to make camp.

She knew what Bran wanted: to hear her beg for his forgiveness. But Leanna vowed privately he would get no such satisfaction, and she held her tongue. Even when he ordered her fed from the same carrion as went to the hounds, she held her tongue. She kicked the platter the watchmen brought her into the dirt, feeding on thoughts of vengeance instead.

Bran did not beat her that night. He drank his fill of wine from an earthenware jug and stared at her moodily for a time, until the sight of her disgusted him. He threw the jug at her then, missing by a hairsbreadth, and stormed from the tent without a word. After an hour passed and he did not return, Leanna tried fitfully to sleep. The cold night air woke her several times with a shiver.

As she struggled against the cold, Leanna slowly became aware of shouting and the sounds of frantic men. The entrance to the pavilion flew open and she was momentarily blinded by torchlight that seemed to explode into the tent.

"What is it?" she asked, recognizing Bran behind the firelight, his face panic-stricken. "What has happened?"

"Loriel is attacking!" Bran shouted. He thrust his torch into a nearby brazier.

Leanna reeled at the news, her heart beating swiftly with fresh hope. She concealed her excitement and watched as Bran raged inside the tent. He threw the furnishings about without regard, frantically searching for something.

A man clad in an undertunic and hose, but bearing a sword and shield, ran into the tent.

"My lord, Duke Loriel's outriders have breached our camp," he gasped. "Our men are taken by surprise. Lest we can muster them, all will be lost."

"Return to your post!" Bran bellowed, his eyes wild. "Organize the ranks. I shall lead us to victory against this feeble rabble. Now go!" He resumed his frenzied search.

"You are undone, Bran," Leanna heard herself say. The days of torment endured at the hands of her captor filled her with an unexpected courage. "If Loriel attacks you, it can only mean that all of Wareham's lords are prepared to rise against you. No one can help you now, not even your barbarian allies."

"You dare?" Bran shouted, and in that moment he found the object he had been seeking. It was the bone-handled knife that slipped from his belt while he had lounged in his wine cups earlier. He advanced on Leanna, blade flashing in the torchlight.

She bit her lip so she would not cry out with fear.

"I will yet defeat that lickspittle, Loriel." Bran's frenzy mounted. "He can slaughter this army to a man, for all I care. It is lost to me already, fit only as a diversion while I return to the safety of Karvoie. I will levy another army, and muster aid from Lorccan's quarter. This is but a mere delay of the inevitable."

He yanked Leanna roughly by the hair and twisted her face upwards. His blade came up and pressed against the soft flesh of her exposed throat. It hovered there, and when Leanna met his stare, she could see terror and madness dancing in his eyes.

"When the enemy takes this pavilion, I shall have set my feet on the road to victory, and you, dear Leanna, will be little more than a memory."

Leanna screamed when Bran's knife lashed out in the gloom. In the deathly silence that followed, the rope binding her to the pole fell, severed, to the ground.

Chapter Twelve

They galloped toward Karvoie, Leanna seated unceremoniously before Bran in the saddle of his giant stallion. Six of Bran's bannermen rode escort, and the group thundered at such breakneck speed Leanna feared she would be thrown from the saddle at any instant. Bran tightened his hold on her with one arm while he guided his steed with the other.

Bran had come within a heartbeat of killing her in his pavilion. Leanna had seen his thoughts clearly as his blade hesitated at her throat; he would rather see her dead in the dust than admit defeat. But there was something else. Something that surprised her. He could not suffer the thought of her in the arms of another. Was it possible that Bran loved her, in his fashion? She had never thought it possible and certainly it would not have made a difference to her; Bran was a monster. His crimes were too vile and too numerous to be redeemed by mere sentiment. If he loved her, Leanna decided, the knowledge was perhaps her greatest weapon.

The rising sun was barely a hint of golden crescent when they entered a thickly wooded area. Through the boughs, Leanna could see the ruins of a monastery thrusting up from a hilltop like jagged fingers. She started at the distinctive slice and thrum of bowshots from behind.

As Bran reined in his mount and wheeled it around, she saw that two of their escort had crashed to the dusty ground. The crimson-shafted quarrels that protruded from them at gruesome angles snapped with the violence of impact. Suddenly, and as if by some enchantment, men appeared from the thicket on either side of the road.

Leanna drew a sharp breath when she saw Emric stride to the center of the road. A dozen men, crossbows held high at the ready, swarmed around him. Naked steel was plain in his hand, and his eyes burned with an inner fire. He was the most beautiful sight Leanna had ever beheld.

"I see the Heldanners failed to end your bothersome life, brother," Bran said with contempt. He spat into the dirt at their feet.

Leanna struggled against Bran's hold and he fought to control his steed. Emric took a step forward as the rest of Bran's guard lowered their weapons in surrender.

"I knew you would flee to Karvoie if Loriel challenged your advance," Emric said. "For all your bluster, you are little more than a base coward. There is no escape now. Release Leanna and join your men."

Bran cast about him. Seeing no alternative, he lowered Leanna slowly to the ground.

She rushed into Emric's arms.

An exaltation the likes of which she had never known filled her as he embraced her. She gripped him tightly, needing to assure herself that he was real and not some specter born of desire. All she had suffered in the last days vanished like chaff on the wind of Emric's gentle kisses.

"Now you will bring me to justice, I presume," Bran interrupted. He was smiling, though there was no humor in the expression.

"That is a privilege you do not deserve," Emric said icily. "You cannot know how many have died and suffered by your hand. And our father . . . To what avail, brother?"

"I did what was necessary. Do you think I did not see you scheming for the throne? That I did not see Loriel's rivalry?" He made a harsh sound in his throat. "Did you believe I would simply allow you the succession?"

"You are mad," Emric whispered, so quietly only Leanna heard him. "Dismount," he ordered.

Bran complied, for the crossbows leveled at him brooked no argument.

Emric ushered Leanna into the protective arms of one of his men. "Now, draw your blade."

"What?" Leanna broke free and seized Emric's arm.

"He must die, Leanna, here and now, and by my hand."

"No," Leanna pleaded, clutching at him desperately. "No, not now that we have been reunited. I thought you dead, but my prayers have been answered." The words tumbled from her mouth. "Let the headsman at Brimhall make justice, but do not place yourself in danger again, I beg you."

"I love you with all my heart and soul, Leanna." Emric touched her cheek. "But I cannot allow my brother to live a moment longer without atoning for the evil he has wrought." Gently, he pried her fingers from him.

"Do not intervene." Emric said to his men-at-arms. "My honor will be satisfied only after I am victorious in single combat." He waited until the ranking sergeant nodded acknowledgment, then shifted back to face his brother.

"Let us cross steel, Bran."

Bran tore his sword free with a snarl and leaped at Emric. His blade flashed like summer lightning, feinting toward the legs, then slashing upward. Dull orange sparks shimmered as blow after blow fell on Emric's blade, forcing him away from the escort.

Leanna watched in horror as the two men fought in grim silence, grunting with the fury of their strokes. Terror flashed through her when Bran's blade ripped across Emric's thigh. Blood gushed to Emric's ankle, but the two men fought on. The sound of steel against steel seemed to fuel their ferocity.

Emric pressed his brother with a series of powerful lunges, barely pulling his sword back in time to parry. The men locked blades for a tense moment, then Bran twisted his wrist in an expert motion, smashing the hilt of his weapon against Emric's unprotected temple.

The prince reeled, his senses still weakened by the wound he had received at the hands of King Lorccan. His grip slackened, releasing the blade, and he fell, struggling against unconsciousness.

Tearing at the fastening of the whip laced to his belt, Bran was upon him in the passing of a heartbeat. The lash encircled Emric's neck in a fatal embrace, and Bran tightened it relentlessly.

"This is my vengeance, dear brother," Bran hissed in Emric's ear. "You were a fool to let me live. I will yet be king and Leanna will be my consort."

Emric fought the darkness descending upon him. His lungs burned and panic rose within him, stealing the last of his breath. His pulse pounded thickly in his temples. He was dying. Dying by Bran's hand . . . like their father. His vision dimmed.

"Bran, my love . . ." Leanna called in a clear voice.

Bran turned to face her with a start, bewilderment plain on his face.

"Leanna?" he said almost as a supplicant, heedless that the deadly circle made by the whip slackened the span of the merest breath.

Emric thrust his head backward, feeling the snap of bone as it connected with Bran's nose. The whip was cast loose as Bran collapsed, and Emric's body heaved uncontrollably to find air at last.

Emric struggled to his feet, scooping up Bran's discarded blade from the dust. With a forceful yell, he raised the sword and sent it down. It shivered through the air and found its mark in a soul as dark as night.

The lash encircled Emris's neck in a fatal embrace, and Bran tightened it relentlessly.

It shivered through the air and found its mark in a soul as dark as night.

Bran's head rolled to a stop three strides from where his body lay.

Emric fell back weakly and Leanna rushed to her beloved, cradling his head to her breast.

"Emric . . . thank God," she whispered, stroking her hand down his face, watching as the anger and strain that marked his features in battle slowly receded. The whip had cut fiercely into the skin of his neck. She did not feel the exultation she expected as she looked at Bran's body and saw the fruit her vengeance. There was only relief. Relief for her and Wareham, and her beloved Emric.

She bent down to kiss the prince and was surprised to find he had passed into unconsciousness. His breath was shallow and ragged, and the color fled his cheeks. Ominous black veins were visible around the edge of the wound in his thigh as his passion's blood drained from him.

When she looked at Bran's blade, she saw the edge was coated in thick, dark oil. She shuddered, her triumph turning to bile in her throat.

Chapter Thirteen

Leanna pressed her lips lightly to Emric's forehead. Fever had made his skin shockingly hot. She dabbed at him with a cloth wrung from a bucket of cold well water.

The poison coating Bran's blade had taken an awful toll. Already Emric was so frail Leanna had to listen at his chest to assure herself he still breathed.

Emric's men-at-arms had built a makeshift litter by lashing together spears and bedrolls, and had carried the prince to the shelter of the ancient cloister they had ridden past earlier. Most of the roof had crumbled long ago, but shelter could still be found in the far section of the wall that remained standing. The old well was partially clogged, but one of the men succeeded in drawing a bucket of clear water. They laid the stricken prince on a bed of blankets and sent riders out to find a healer.

That had been hours ago.

Leanna pressed his hands against her heart while she studied his face, wondering if she would ever see the raging thunder in those magical green eyes again. Would she ever drown in them as she had done so many times in the past? Her heart pounding with fear, she knelt at his side.

"Don't leave me, Emric. Don't leave me now," she pleaded as if words alone might keep him alive. She wished for Mirabel and her medicine pouch.

The sun was setting slowly through the age-worn arches, where stained glass had once presided, and the ruddy light of the campfire lent Emric's pallid body some color. Leanna lay down beside him.

His body, usually so sensual, was now diminished by the wantonness of the poison within him. The dark wound below his hip had angry patterns of scarlet tracing across his belly and groin. He groaned with some horrific nightmare.

"Do you remember, love, the first time you came to me?" she whispered to soothe him. If the men sitting about the fire could hear her whispers, they gave no indication.

"You loosened the ribbons that held my chemise and slipped it from my shoulders; you always did like those blue ribbons. I laughed, for you looked at me as though you were afraid to touch me." She smiled at the memory. "I looked into your eyes and knew that I could trust you with my body . . . with my heart. Remember, my love? I kissed your fingertips, and when you placed your hand against my breast, my heart beat so wildly I thought it would take flight."

Leanna leaned closer to his ear and continued. "You were careful, my love, and gentle." She kissed him lightly, hoping to see a flicker of movement from his dark eyelashes.

There was a polite cough. One of Emric's bondsmen approached with a bowl of steaming broth.

"You have not eaten today, my lady. It will do the prince no service if you fall ill, as well." He set the bowl down near the makeshift bed.

She thanked him and ate a bit, but Emric's body seemed to heat still more with fever so she put the bowl aside.

Leanna tended Emric as best she could for long hours into the night. At some point, exhaustion overcame her and she fell into slumber at the side of her beloved.

Her head came up suddenly. The sleeping men around the fire snored and the lookout walked his perimeter as before, but the air had a strangely languid quality. When she gazed at Emric, he looked as he did that day in the meadow outside Brimhall: restive but strong, healthy, and full of vigor.

She knew at once that she was dreaming, though she did not recall ever having a

"You loosened the ribbons that held my
chemise and slipped it from my shoulders; you
always did like those blue ribbons."

Leanna tended Emric as best she could for long hours into the night.

dream so lucid. There was a flutter of wings, and when Leanna turned to investigate, she saw a robed figure approaching.

Leanna gasped when she recognized her mother, Ursanne.

"Oh, Mother." Tears rushed to Leanna's eyes as they embraced. The weariness and pain of the last days flowed from her. "How I have missed you."

Though she understood she was dreaming, the clarity and power of her emotions struck Leanna with awe.

"And I have missed you, Lea." Her mother gently touched Leanna's cheek.

Leanna stared. She had almost forgotten the name by which her mother had called her as a child.

Ursanne looked at Emric, who lay near them on the pallet. "Who is this man?"

"Emric, the king," Leanna said, then added, ". . . and my betrothed."

"Do you love him?" Ursanne asked with a gentle concern.

"Yes, Mother, above all else."

"Then why do you let him die?"

"I . . . I do not understand," Leanna stammered.

"Child, give me your hand." Her mother's voice echoed in the space around them. "You have the power . . . as you have always had it, for it was yours even before your birth.

"O Mother! O Maiden! O Goddess!" Ursanne began to speak the ancient vow of Druid priestesses, which she had recited so often in years past. "Goddess of the Light, hearken to thy daughters. Grant thy power and thy wisdom, and in thy wisdom, grant sight, the Ningal, so that thy will be done. O Mother! O Maiden! O Goddess! Hear thy daughters' oath: be true to the Queen of Light. True to Earth and Sea and Sky. Be true to thine own Self besides. True to Love above all else."

Leanna shivered as her mother completed the ancient oath.

"True to Love above all else." It had been so long since she said the words that she had forgotten the end of the verse.

As her mind struggled to come to terms with the implications, she realized

Ursanne had spoken without vocalizing. She used the Ningal to communicate as she did years ago in their private moments together.

Leanna closed her eyes. There was a peace within her she hadn't felt in a long time. When she looked about again, Ursanne was gone.

"Mother?" she cried.

From the void she heard Ursanne's voice calling her name softly.

"Lady Leanna?"

One of the men-at-arms shook her awake gently. Leanna opened her eyes. The dream had been so real, so compelling. She thought she could still hear the echo of her mother's voice.

"It's the prince, my lady." The man spoke with difficulty, his bearded face lined with worry. "He has . . . during the night . . ."

Leanna's heart lurched, and she turned toward Emric, reaching out to touch his pale cheek. Instead of the fever that had burned his skin, he now felt so very cold.

"No!" she cried, scrambling to her knees.

She pressed her ear to Emric's lips, then to his heart, listening for a sign of life, but finding none. Her mind recoiled from thoughts too painful to bear. This was a nightmare from which there would be no awakening.

Leanna placed her hands on his chest; she bade his heart to begin beating again. There had always been reservation within her toward Emric, despite the love that she bore him, for he had been forced into her life by the will of other men. Only now that he lay cold beneath her did she realize the purity of her love for him. It did not matter what had brought them together.

The Goddess was a goddess of light. Her gift was the Ningal, the sight that revealed the light of life in all men. It could not be dimmed. It could not be blinded, even by the curtain of death.

"No," she cried again, fighting the grief welling up from inside her. "You cannot die. You must live!"

She recited her mother's words: *I am true to the Queen of Light. True to Earth and*

Instead of the fever that had burned his skin, he now felt so very cold.

Sea and Sky. I am true to my own Self besides. True to Love above all else!

A wave of serenity swept over her. Leanna pressed her hand over Emric's wound. She let her love for him flow unrestrained until a sensation of heat infused her. The Ningal grew from within her mind, filling her with light. A mystical awareness of the world around her grew and she directed it to Emric.

The magic she wrought rushed through him, and a sound, half cry, half moan, issued from his lips. His chest rose fully for the first time since the poisoned blade touched him. His green eyes opened, and he whispered her name.

Tears of joy streamed down Leanna's face. She leaned down to Emric, covering his mouth with hers.

Emric returned her kiss, and she knew that all would be well at last.

He had fallen in battle a prince.

He awoke in Leanna's arms a king.

End

Cherif Fortin

Lynn Sanders

Cherif Fortin is a freelance photographer, illustrator, and writer living in Chicago, Illinois. At one time he has worked as a professional stuntman, as a full-time firefighter, and as one of the country's leading romance cover models. Cherif's artwork has been featured on the covers of hundreds of books in dozens of countries, and on calendars and collectibles. He runs the successful Fortin & Sanders Studio along with partner, Lynn Sanders, producing commercial art and photography for leading clients internationally. He lives with his wife, Dawn, and their three children: Kira, Kai, and Lara.

Lynn Sanders is an artist, photographer, and writer of romance fiction and children's books. She is co-owner of Fortin & Sanders Studio, which produces cover art for some of the top publishers in the world. Her paintings have been exhibited at Epcot Center and are owned by private collectors such as Hugh Hefner and Fabio. She has three adult children, three grandchildren, and one great-grandchild. She lives in northern Illinois with Ce Ce, her faithful Cirneco dell Etna.

Visit Lynn and Cherif online at www.fortinandsanders.com.

For more information about other
great titles from Medallion Press, visit

medallionpress.com